AMERICAN LION

Professor Tim Rush teaches graduate and undergraduate courses in literacy education, humanities education, and linguistics at the University of Wyoming. Working closely with the tribes of the Wind River Indian Reservation, he has helped develop UW programs for certifying teachers of American Indian children. He was awarded the University of Wyoming Outreach School's *Holon Family Award* and was recognized by the International Reading Association with its Jerry Johns Outstanding Teacher Educator in Reading Award. Grandfather of a girls' volleyball champion and two young men serving in the US Air Force, Tim Rush lives on th .... of L....... Wyoming, with .... and an array of horse .... from the wild k ...

First published by GemmaMedia in 2015.

GemmaMedia
230 Commercial Street
Boston MA 02109 USA

www.gemmamedia.com

Printed in the United States of America
978-1-936846-53-5

Library of Congress Cataloging-in-Publication Data

Rush, R. Timothy.
   American lion / R. Timothy Rush.
      pages cm. — (Gemma Open Door)
   ISBN 978-1-936846-53-5
1. Puma—Anecdotes. 2. Human-animal relationships—
Anecdotes. I. Title.
   QL737.C23R87 2015
   599.75'24—dc23

                                              2015035877

Cover by Laura Shaw Design

Inspired by the Irish series designed for new readers, Gemma's Open Doors provide fresh stories, new ideas, and essential resources for young people and adults as they embrace the power of reading and the written word.

Brian Bouldrey
North American Series Editor

GEMMA

Open Door

For Alice

Contents

A Solitary Hunter

I am a solitary hunter. I live and hunt alone, but I am not lonely. Nature put me here for a purpose. I provide balance. I live to hunt and hunt to live. To live, I must kill. I am very good at it. Silently, swiftly, almost painlessly, my prey falls to me. Four-legged creatures of all sizes, from mice to horses, are my prey. On rare occasions, two-leggeds like you—your brothers, your sisters, or your young—have fallen to my sharp fangs and claws.

When I am near, you never know. When you are near, I always know. I know your language, but you have forgotten mine. I read you with more than my eyes. You speak to me in scent, sound, and movement. Your words mean little to me. Their tone and music mean much more. Your chatter draws me to you. Your silence tells me "stop."

Naturally, my animal cousins fear me. However, you and your kind hate me. Two-legged humans are the only animals who can hate. Did you know that?

Once I am a full-grown, 150-pound giant cat, only two-leggeds, with their little wolf friends, dare hunt me.

I am like a baby when I am young. My mother cares for me. She feeds me, protects me, and teaches. We sleep in high, sheltered dens away from our enemies—such as you and your kind—and stay near those who nourish us.

Two years. That is all that I share with my kin. My sisters have the gift of *motherhood and family. But he-lions must go life alone.*

And after four, five, or six years alone, my life of hunting and balancing is done.

Introduction:
View from a Window

The lion walked calmly across the wooden footbridge, as relaxed and confident as a house cat. He weighed 150 pounds and stretched eight feet from tip of nose to tail. His coat was thick and the color of strong coffee. The hair around his mouth and eyes was lighter, like coffee with lots of cream in it. His ears were small and rounded. A four-foot-long tail waved gently above and behind him. He was beautiful and scary *big*.

The cat was stealthy in a natural and graceful way. No one saw him but me that early May morning, though there were thirty people nearby. He was a silent and invisible spirit to them.

He turned off the bridge and padded softly through the grass toward the cabin window where I stood. He seemed to look into my eyes. Then he vanished. Yep, disappeared! I dashed to other windows, then, in a stupid move, stepped outside the cabin. No sign. I looked at the roof and in trees and bushes nearby. No lion.

If I had known more about the mountain lion, I would never have left that cabin while he was near. The truth is, although I have lived in lion country for most of my seventy-odd years, this was the first and only "real-life" lion I had seen. Most people in the Rocky Mountain range, from the southern tip of South America to northern Canada, have never seen a cougar. Sightings are very rare, even at a distance, let alone up close and personal, like mine.

Later in the morning, I talked with the cowboy who lived on and managed the ranch where I was staying. He told me that several deer had been killed by lions over the winter.

"Last year we saw a female lion with two cubs several times," he told me. "They are killing the deer. The mother raised them on the ranch, and they have no fear of humans. Their last kill was almost on my front porch." He went on, a little sadly, "I guess we'll have to do something about them soon."

I knew what he meant by *something*—bullets. But why?

A couple of facts I learned: Mountain

lions are not really lions. They are closer to your house cat, the bobcat, and the lynx than to the African lion and his American cousin, the jaguar. And they do not always live in the mountains. That is why this animal (*Puma concolor*) is called by different names—puma, panther, cougar, catamount, cat of the mountains—in different parts of our country. They have been spotted as far east as Connecticut in the last few years.

What follows are real-life experiences told in the voices of my Westerner friends who have had encounters with mountain lions. The first one is another story of my own. It helps me remember that lions are much more than killers in the wild.

ONE

Predator and Prey

On winter nights, when I step outside the house to get fuel for the fireplace or check on the horses, I hear things. Sometimes it is the crunch of snow under my boots. Other times, the sounds are far more interesting. The call of a coyote is one of my favorites.

The Plains Indian tribes respect all animals, but honor the coyote for its cunning. In their stories, the coyote is a selfish trickster who fools people, other animals, and always, himself. In real life, the coyote finds and takes prey by pretending to be friendly. Trickery.

*   *   *

Now and then, I hear the sound of many coyote voices. On one late evening during the yearly thaw that follows the Christmas season, the yipping, yapping, yammering chorus told me there were many and that they were happy and not far off. They had caught something and were going to eat well.

"Maybe an antelope?" I thought to myself. Young or old, weak pronghorn must be rare kills for these rodent-hunting coyotes.

Unlike mountain lions, coyotes work in pairs or packs. Since I've never seen them hunt, I imagine that these sixty-pound canines fan out and scout alone. When one finds a big prey animal or a carcass, coyotes nearby are called with yippy-yappy barks or high-pitched howls. To those who haven't heard this singing before, the coyotes sound like they are playing. The "funny" chatter, coming from the ramshackle buildings of the abandoned homestead nearby, is what I heard that night.

As they gathered for the kill, their barking became more threatening and chilling. Mixed in with all the chatter, I was sure I heard yowls and growls that were not part of coyote vocabulary. I listened with a shiver.

An hour later, I went to check on the four horse friends that I feed daily and ride weekly. The coyote ruckus was still going on. Their voices were more urgent and serious. Experience told me that, like people, coyotes get quiet once they start feeding. This pack was not eating. Not yet. They were killing just far enough away from me to be hidden in darkness. They must have picked out something big. I walked faster to see about my ponies. They were fine, all standing at the fence, famished expressions on their faces.

I scattered a coffee can of packer cubes and walked toward the house, wondering what was happening out of sight in those tumbledown sheds and darkened barns.

The next morning, I put a leash on Buddy, my big, spotted hunting dog, and we squeezed between the wooden rails of the crossbuck fence. Soon we found what the coyotes had happened on. A pair of yearling mountain lions who'd strayed from their mother's protection.

From the tracks in the snow, I imagined that fight through the young lions' eyes.

"Brother and I were hungry. Two days had passed since Mother had slipped under the river ice and left us orphans. Hunting all day on our own, we found the picked-over remains of an antelope beside the hard black trail. While we were gnawing at bones and hide, a coyote came and stood still, watching us.

Darkness came, and the coyote gave three sharp barks. Very soon his mate arrived, and together they moved closer, both barking now and then. Two coyotes were pests. Brother and I ate, tearing at the carcass.

When we finished, we looked up into many bright coyote eyes. They were all around, in front and back of us, creeping closer.

Each little wolf was nearly our size. Brother and I knew the threat. We looked to get above these little wolves. There was a fence of thin logs. We sprang to it and knew it was not high enough. We ran along its top rail to a little empty barn and leapt to its flat, metal roof, feeling it give under our weight. We hunched there, waiting for the fight. The coyotes tried again and again to jump from the fence to the roof of the old shed. Again and again they slipped and fell, yipping like scared puppies. Twice our claws slapped down on their noses and helped them to fall.

But the standoff lasted only a short while. The little wolves jumped from the fence and joined us on the roof of the shed. We held our own, sending coyotes off the roof, yelping in pain. Then the roof collapsed beneath us and we fell together into a swarm of snarling, tearing meat-eaters."

Instinct had told the cubs to climb away from danger. All they could find were the top rails of the wooden fence, about five feet off the ground. Not high enough. The rickety shed was not tall enough, either. They were cornered by half a dozen or more hungry canines who matched them in size and outclassed them in experience. The outcome was set before the struggle started.

Questions crashed together in my mind. Mountain lions, almost in my back yard?

How could this be? Mountain lions are at the top of the food chain.

The answers came through my neighbor's experience a week later.

TWO

Charlie Jansen's Barn Cat

Charlie Jansen's ranch is the last place I'd look for mountain lions. Flat. Not even a hill on the place and hardly a tree in sight. No place for mountain lions. Right.

Charlie is a sturdy, good-sized rancher who raises beef cattle on the high-level plains east of the Medicine Bow range. Around here, in the 1980s—when people still read newspapers—he made the front page of our local paper when one of his cows had a two-headed calf. The reporter and photographer came knocking on his door. Quite a commotion followed, but it gradually tailed off as families and schoolteachers lost interest. The ranch soon returned to being a quiet place out on the windswept "baldies."

For eight months, the snow had fallen, melted, and fallen again. The prairie wind had whistled and roared, pounded and hammered almost daily. There had been only three or four days of below-zero temperatures, but Charlie had marked the kitchen calendar the morning the backyard thermometer had reached minus forty-four degrees. After forty-five years on the ranch where he grew up, he took it all in stride. The high-centered pickup? Charlie shoveled and winched it out. The frozen water line at the stock tank? Charlie fixed it. The cow that bogged in the mud at the pond? Charlie roped and pulled it out from horseback.

There were no surprises in the rhythm of ranching. But, in a space between the hay bales in the barn loft, something completely amazing was going on, as Charlie was about to find out.

On a windy, late-winter Friday morning around breakfast time, a-came a knock on the back door. Charlie looked out at the official Wyoming Game and Fish Department pickup truck idling beside his own, headlights shining. A short, stout, uniformed man in a green, hooded parka stood on the porch.

"What's up, Billy?" Charlie smiled. He was always glad to have company. Billy Brown had worked with the Bureau of Land Management for many years. He was a sort of legend in the county. "Come on in. Coffee's fresh-hot. Not often we get to see each other. What brings you out here?"

"Well, I brought a couple friends from the university."

"UWs always welcome. Wave them on in." Charlie smiled again.

The headlights went out as the engine switched off. A young man and woman got out and walked into the kitchen. Billy quickly explained that both were wildlife management professors and researchers. They had been doing fieldwork all week in the national forest, checking animals they had tagged with radio collars over the last two or three years.

Charlie was curious. "What are you tracking?"

Tom, the university man, replied, "Several species. The easy ones are hibernating. Bears, mostly. But it is one of the more difficult ones that brings us here. She's one that Cheryl here is studying."

Billy interrupted. "The reason we are here is an old mama lion, a mountain lion. You know, puma, cougar. Old-time Texans called 'em panthers."

"Yes," Cheryl piped up. "Mountain lion. She's living in your barn. I think she has a kitten or two."

"What?" Charlie almost laughed. "That's not possible! I am in that barn five times a day. Not a footprint or any sign. No lions in there!"

"Well, maybe not—I doubt you're on the alert for cougars. But she's been there—her radio collar is transmitting from there. Weak signal, after two years, but it's coming from the barn."

"Maybe, but lions avoid people and the nearest real wilderness is twenty miles away," Charlie reminded them. "And a lion would be taking my calves."

"Lions prefer deer," said Cheryl. "You have plenty of those out here in the brush and marshes. I saw that muley bunch with the deformed ears on the drive in from the pavement."

"That's true enough." Charlie stood up. "Let's get out to that barn. I am getting muddled."

Fifty yards of walking took them to the barn door. Everyone knew to be quiet.

"My barn," Charlie muttered to himself. "If it weren't for that radio collar, I'd bet money."

Cheryl calmly took charge as Charlie swung the big door open and the four entered the darkness of the old two-story building.

"This receiver tells me she's here, but not exactly where," she said in a quiet voice.

"What's your best guess?" Billy asked.

Tom pointed toward the half-empty hayloft and Cheryl nodded yes. She stepped softly under the loft.

Charlie had brought out a big flashlight and he now handed it to the young woman. She shone it along the rough-cut boards above her head, then stopped and smiled at the others. "Right there," she seemed to say.

Charlie thought he heard movement from above and saw scraps of hay filtering down from between the boards. Cheryl removed her heavy coat and went to the ladder.

"You going to go up there with her?" Charlie questioned.

"Got to." She smiled. "It's my work."

In ten seconds, she had gracefully ascended the board rungs of the old ladder and was muttering soothing words into a certain place in the darkness. Then she shone the beam of light. But not where she looked.

Charlie Jansen felt his heart pounding. A 100-pound *girl*—by his sixty-year-old standards—was up there with an adult female lion that might weigh 140. And there could be cubs to protect.

"She going to use a tranquilizer?"

Tom answered in a whisper. "No,

just try to get a good look. See if the cat looks healthy and uninjured."

Above, Cheryl moved the light so that it shone on the lioness's tawny coat and reflected from her yellow eyes. The cat remained impassive, offering a purry sort of growl once or twice. But the woman didn't push her by closing in. She made a few mental notes on the cat's condition and slowly crawled back and away.

"Well, she seems in good shape," Cheryl reported when she was back down on the floor. "Well fed, so your deer population is being controlled. Odd, though, she's been swimming. The air up there smells like wet cat."

"Any babies?" asked Tom.

"None, and she's not pregnant. She

is between litters. Probably just finished the process of driving off a mature cub or two. A good thing for you and for us, Mr. Jansen."

The young professors explained that had cubs been present, it would have been necessary to catch them and transport them with their mother from the Jansen ranch to a site somewhere in the mountains.

Charlie caught on. "'Necessary' means I'd have started missing my calves and that capturing lions can be, er, 'interesting'?"

Everyone chuckled.

Well, the way this had turned out was just about perfect for the next several weeks. No one on hand that winter morning, two- or four-legged, was hurt or even threatened. Charlie and all kept close tabs on the guest in the barn. He even gave her a name. "Liz'beth," he'd call up to her as he entered the barn each day. Some days, he thought she answered with her purry growl. Until one morning during spring lambing, the growl and the lion were gone.

The next day, a red Ford pickup stopped in the yard. Charlie saw Garrick Shaw's .30-30 Winchester propped beside him in the cab and knew.

"Looky, in the truck bed," called Garrick with pride. "See what I caught stalking my ewes around sunset last night!"

THREE

Jake and Duke: The Rock Creek Lion Fight

Jake Hall is a fine young man—cowboy, hunter, construction foreman. Also quiet, humble, fearless, and a friend to all. And most especially, Jake is a fisherman. Most of the qualities and skills that his tribe prizes were inherited by Jake Hall.

Jake knows about mountain lions firsthand. And a lot of what he knows was learned in Rock Creek Canyon on a summer day in the last years of the twentieth century. A hungry cougar and his sheepdog, Duke, were his teachers . . .

*   *   *

Biologists write that the closest relative to the big lions of Africa and Eurasia is the jaguar. African lions hunt their prey in groups. Mountain lions hunt alone. Jake knows the feeling of being stalked by a lone killer far from any kind of help.

It was a summer Saturday when he decided to hike his favorite stream in the "Bows" west of Laramie. He'd worked a construction site at the University of Wyoming all during the week. Long twelve-hour days—Jake was ready for time with Mother Nature. In fact, he and old Duke were always ready for time in the mountains.

Jake put his fly-fishing gear behind the seat of the pickup truck he called "the War Pony" and threw in his lunch box and coffee thermos. Duke hopped in beside him. Best friends.

Jake told me about the day like this:

"Duke lived up to his name that day. I named him for John Wayne—strong, silent, with a 'no-quit attitude,' and just mean enough. Gentle, but always ready for a fight.

"We headed for Rock Creek Canyon, back then, about the prettiest and lonesome-est place around. It was rugged and rocky. The creek poured down from the high mountains, but there were plenty of nice trout holes, if you were willing to work. We always were.

"That canyon made you work for its fish. The rocky trail winds through big boulders. You had to scramble over those jagged rocks to get to the best holes.

"Duke liked to nose around, but he always kept me in sight. I guess he thought I'd get into some kind of trouble. Then he'd come a-running to help. Hmm." Jake looked down and smiled softly.

"Well, we hiked up the canyon about a mile before the fishing started, caught a nice brookie right off. Then we started moving down toward the mouth of the canyon.

"I was all concentration. Between the fishing and watching my footing in the rocks I didn't notice much else. After an hour or so, I had two more nice trout in my creel. I sat down at the grassy brink of the stream and took a break. This was a good day.

"Duke wasn't interested in my PB-

and-J sandwich. He just sat beside me looking at the water flash by. Then he dropped to his belly and tensed up, in that Aussie shepherd way. He seemed ready to fight.

"I scanned the opposite bank where he was looking. Coyote? Badger? Marmot? I didn't see anything but rocks and grass and trees. I took a bite of an apple. Did I say, Duke liked to eat the cores?

"Then Duke started his 'this-is-serious' growl. Still, I saw nothing. The growl became a rasping snarl. I squinted hard and saw it—a mountain lion. His sandy grey color, exactly like the ten-foot-high boulder where he was crouched.

"I tell you, that cat was only a few feet from where my next steps were taking me. He might have had me for lunch.

"I reached for Duke's collar. But I was half a second too late. In a blur, he cleared the creek in one bound and dodged through the rocks. The lion sat up and leaned back, ready to slice the dog with the razor hooks of a huge paw.

"Now, when Duke was six months old, he ate a bucket of elk guts. I swear, he doubled his size in a week. So he was no typical shepherd dog. Duke was a ninety-pound fighting dog with a shepherd's instincts to protect his flock.

"Still, that lion probably outweighed him by seventy pounds. If the cat had surprised the dog, Duke would have had no chance. But, ha-ha, this day, it was the lion that was surprised.

"That old speckled dog topped that ledge and slammed into the cat before any paws could swipe! Duke's teeth got a good hold on the lion. The lion wrapped his front legs around the snarling dog, and off the ledge they rolled. Eight feet down! They slammed the ground. Duke was dazed for a second, then jumped to the attack. But the cat was smart and quick. In a flash, he sprang—not at the dog, but back up to the ledge. Then away into the brush.

"My adrenalin was up, too, I guess. I was across the water and caught Duke's collar before he could chase. Man, a ninety-pound dog, in attack mode, is a handful. I was lucky. Duke was sensible and didn't bite me in the confusion.

"We crossed the creek and Duke got a whole apple as his reward. Lots of good words and petting, too.

"We sat for a while and both calmed down. It was barely two minutes from the first growl till it was all over. I checked Duke over for wounds—not a scratch. He panted and looked at me with those crazy blue eyes. I believe he was proud and happy.

"Somehow, I didn't feel much like fishing. We followed the trail down, toward my truck. After a couple hundred yards I sat down for a rest. Duke flopped down, too.

"I guess I nodded off, because the sound of my dog's snarling bark startled me. That cat must have been hungry. He'd walked right up to us. Twenty feet away (a lion can jump that far), tensed and ready to spring, was the puma. He was ready for business. Why hadn't I packed the .45 Ruger Vaquero I kept under the driver's seat?

"Well, Duke made his move again, and this time the lion sprang back into the rocks. 'Duke, here!!' I called, loud as I could. He turned and came to me. 'All right, let's get away from here.'

"I bet I had my head turned around backward half the time as I stumbled down the trail. Seemed certain that lion would try again. He just needed the right ambush.

"If that cat had wanted dog, or me, for supper, he reconsidered. Duke had taught the lion and me that an Aussie shepherd can make a meal more work than it is worth. And we didn't see the lion anymore. That was just fine with me, but Duke seemed depressed and disappointed for about a week."

Well, that is Jake Hall's story. It rings true with what I have read since. The lesson of that day is this: if you get the chance, it is best to fight and drive the attacker away. Sticks, stones, or a big, brave, dog are recommended.

In fact, it seems that Jake was in little danger. It was his fearless dog, Duke, that cougar was hunting.

FOUR

Ryan, Riann, and the Guardian Mare

Ryan Mays is one of those young men who give me hope for the future. Only age twenty-one, he is strong, smart, and willing to do any job and do it well. By hand, and working alone, he can load a fifty-five-foot flatbed trailer with hay, eight bales high, in forty-five minutes and never let up or complain. Farmers and ranchers pray for "hands" like Ryan.

I imagine that Riann Riley also prayed for a boy like Ryan. Now I bet she prays words of thanks that he's her beau.

It was fun to see Riann watch Ryan

work with his dad and me that last time I loaded hay on his place south of Kinnear on the Wind River Indian Reservation. It was more than fun to hear Ol' Stan talk with glowing pride about his cowboy son.

He described the day that they went off riding the buttes and arroyos. Riann rode her new gelding, Cutter, and Ryan his trusty old palomino "kid horse" mare, Yuma. It was early autumn, and the rattlers had settled down in the cool of the evenings.

Not that my young friends had anything to fear from snakes. The main reason for this was Yuma. She was near twenty-five years old, somewhere around seventy in horse years. Long ago she had learned to "sniff out" snakes. She could sense and avoid them almost magically. But the evening of this story, she was to be magical in a more surprising and heroic and deadly way.

You know how it is to work all day in the sun and still be ready for some fun? Fun, like a long ride down an evening trail with your best girl and best horse as twilight is just beginning? And the big full October moon just rising? Ryan and his girl were people like that and this was one of those nights. Beautifully at peace.

Together, they saddled up. Ryan automatically packed against trouble, dropping his old Ruger Vaquero in his saddlebag. Quietly happy, they rode out into the arid badlands without a care.

Yep, it is puzzling how young folks

in love can forget the aches and pains of the day and lose track of time and place, just rolling along to the sounds and rhythms of horse and saddle on a dusty trail through the sagebrush. Even the horses seemed mesmerized.

Cutter was the first to show signs of nervousness. He danced. He balked. He tried to turn against his rider's cues. Ryan spoke to him from his horse and Cutter settled. But there was high tension in his movements.

The couple came to a steep, narrow draw that they had ridden at least once a week for two years and started down. But Cutter balked. He backed, side-stepped, rocked, and hopped. He did everything but buck. When Ryan saw that Riann was spooked by this, he and

Riann traded horses. But the gelding still would not enter the little canyon.

"Don't know what's got into him tonight," he confessed. "Let's ride around the canyon and come down the trail on the far slope."

"Oh, I want to see the moon rise from down in the canyon," pleaded Riann. "I'll ride this old girl down and meet you at the bottom. Okay?"

Ryan couldn't say no to those brown eyes. "All right." He reached over and gave her and the trusty mare each a pat, murmuring low, "Yuma, you be good to her." Then they moved off. Riann rode into the arroyo, Ryan along the rim. Both unsuspecting of any danger.

Ryan concentrated on settling Cutter's nerves. Talking, humming, working the reins and his legs, he reminded the young horse of his training cues. Gradually, both he and Cutter calmed down.

The little canyon was a picture of gray rock and black shadow. Yuma moved with care, ears moving forward and side-to-side. Riann was alert to her mount's movements, knowing the horse's eyes moved in unison with her ears. Both horse and rider knew the place and the trail they rode. Their body language told that they loved where they were and what they were doing. They savored the relaxing, muffled sound of saddle leather, the smell of horse, dust, and sage. The beams of the low-riding moon angled on the canyon walls and ledges. In them, the dust from Yuma's falling hooves rose like little puffy clouds hugging the ground.

"Perfect, isn't it girl?" Riann said in her high, singsong way. "In the whole wide world, how many horses and people are doing this tonight?" She and Yuma seemed to smile together at the words.

The young lion sprang, seeming to float silently downward from his hiding place on the ledge ten feet above. Just as he was about to strike the girl with the full force of his 140 pounds, Yuma bolted sideways.

Riann lost her stirrups at the suddenness of Yuma's move. The lion struck both the girl's arms and Yuma's neck and saddle. In an instant, all three were sprawling on the ground and scrambling in the dust. Their screams, one of surprise, one of fear, and one of frustration, sounded as one. They struggled to their feet in a fog of white dust.

The lion rose first and took aim for the girl, who was now on her knees. She was hunched in pain, her right arm limp and dangling. Blood oozed from her head and shoulder. Dazed, she screamed for Ryan as the hungry lion, eyes gleaming in the moonlight, crouched low and moved to finish his helpless prey.

Ryan patted his alarmed horse at the sound. He knew he was half a mile from the terror he heard in Riann's and Yuma's voices. He could ride hard up the slope and down the canyon or he could ride down the rest of the hill and up the canyon. He spurred the buckskin and down they went.

He knew he was not heading for an accident. Yuma was honest and steady. Riann had been a rider all her life. This was real trouble. He wanted to gallop, but he couldn't risk a stumbling wreck with nervous young Cutter.

They cantered down and left toward the mouth of the little canyon. Every stride seemed in slow motion. More screams rang out above the sound of speeding horse and rider. One of the screams was big cat, not horse or human. Seconds seemed like hours.

Knowing the lion scream and fearing the worst, Ryan reached back for the pistol in his saddlebag. "Damn," he cursed. "The Ruger is on Yuma's saddle!"

At the mouth of the canyon, Ryan turned Cutter in and up. At once, the green buckskin balked and bucked. No time to argue, Ryan swung down. "You son-of-a-gun! You sensed this at the other end. Next time, I . . ." He cut the sentence short and started to sprint up the trail. What he would do when he got to Riann—he didn't know. Throw rocks?

The yellow mare was a prey animal, born to run from the bear, wolf, and cougar. Raising a dust cloud, she scrabbled upright, whirled, and ran. Not away, but straight at the slinking, snarling creature that was poised to strike Riann.

What a sight! The old mare slid to a stop, facing the lion and shielding the wounded girl. Riann scuttled backward and behind a small boulder. Yuma, neck bowed and hooves flashing, stood her ground, kicking clouds of dust and rocks, whinnying and grunting—the sounds of fighting stallions. She seemed like three or four angry studs. Or like a mother mare protecting her foal.

The lion was persistent. Twice he tried to go around the mare. Each time she met him with sharp, stomping, flashing, steel-shod hooves. The lion slashed and the horse bled, but she did not give in.

The noise of the battle reached Ryan when he was a hundred yards down the canyon. It was a lion all right, but the sounds were mainly horse. Angry, protective horse! He rounded the final bend and ran to Riann. She hugged him with her good arm. He turned to go to Yuma and retrieve his .45.

What those young people saw next will never be forgotten. Yuma was on the attack, not with her feet, but with her jaws and teeth!

The old horse struck like a snake. Her head darted out, mouth open eight inches wide, and her long teeth clamped on the lion's neck. She reared back, shook the cat like a dog might shake a rat, and, with a toss of her head, threw it ten feet away. Almost before it touched the ground, she caught it in the same way and shook it again. Then she casually dropped it and, reversing herself, bucked and stomped it hard with her hind feet. The lion did not move.

Nickering and wheezing, the old horse turned from her victim and walked directly to the human masters she had just saved.

Ryan reached for Yuma's reins. She

stood quietly, trembling and breathing hard as her lifelong friend helped the girl up into the saddle. "Can you ride while I lead?" he asked softly. "Or do I need to climb up behind you?"

"I can ride," she replied through clenched teeth and a strained smile, ". . . at a walk."

Slowly, the three started down the dusty path between the steep walls of the narrow little canyon to complete the circle that led home.

Behind them, a battered young cat-of-the-mountains struggled to his feet and, with one paw lifted high, limped off up the trail. He began the twenty-mile trek to the cliffside den that he'd known all his young life, where he would find his mother's aid.

*   *   *

Yuma knew and returned the love of the people she lived with, helped—and protected. Yuma was a caretaker who proved the truth of what the best horsemen know. The Nez Perce people may be our country's finest horsemen. They gaze over small herds in their mountain meadows and say, "There are our horses, who take great care of us."

FIVE

Curiosity and a Cat: Fort Washakie School Playground

Five hundred Eastern Shoshoni schoolchildren play in the shade of the old cottonwood trees at the beautiful Fort Washakie School. The school sits near the river on the western part of the Wind River Indian Reservation in a place called Warm Valley, in the shadow of the Wind River Mountains of Wyoming. Five hundred schoolchildren—and at least one invisible mountain lion.

Not too long before the day this story happened, I heard two Fort Washakie teachers talk of being stalked by a lion as they jogged for evening exercise. One said that she was pushing her two little kids in their stroller when a "hungry-looking" cougar had slunk along behind the four of them. The cougar followed till they got close to a group of teenagers near the school building. Then the lion "disappeared."

People coexist with wildlife in this place. But they get nervous about lions. Dogs and other pets have gone missing, and once in a long while there are sightings of young or adult lions.

But in the willows that run along the river, there are wild things that live lives completely separate from those of their human neighbors. Most of these animals are barely aware of humans. The cougars, deer, and others who live along the river know to be cautious. But they are naturally curious.

There is an old saying about curiosity and cats.

Science tells us that lions are attracted to little children's squealing voices and scurrying antics at play. To these hunting cats, children sometimes seem like little animals in distress—easy prey. Naturally, near schools, there is little tolerance for large predators.

So, if you knew that an old mama lion climbed in darkness each morning to a low branch in a giant cottonwood close to this school—what trouble would you predict?

In Mrs. LeClerq's kindergarten classroom, Billi Ferris and her friends waited for recess. Black eyes and long braids shone in the morning light. After two hours of "work," this was one of their favorite times of day. Right after mid-morning snack, they would pull on their jackets and head for the swings, jungle gyms, and basketball courts.

So far, the morning with Mrs. LeClerq had been great good. She made sure that lessons were fun. That meant that everyone felt proud of the jobs they did, and reading, math, and Shoshone culture were all brought together in one lesson. Mrs. LeClerq loved her kids and she loved being their teacher. Her motto was posted on the front wall in big letters next to the American flag.

It said, "Respect all things. Respect yourself. You are Shoshone. And remember who you represent!" Everyone knew the motto by heart. They knew that it meant they should be kind, courageous, hardworking, cheerful—and all the rest of the thirteen values that made them Shoshone.

The bell chimed softly, many-colored jackets were pulled on, and fourteen happy children lined up at the door. Billi's big sister, Nadine (the classroom assistant), grabbed the big canvas bag of balls, Frisbees, and jump ropes. Then she led everyone out across the wide sidewalk and onto the big grassy playground.

As soon as they reached the grass, all fourteen voices erupted in a high-pitched roar.

*   *   *

Mama lion was unnoticeable on the thick branch where she lay relaxed and waiting. To her, the children on the playground far below were simply interesting, darting around in their many-colored, shiny skins. Ants on an anthill might fascinate you in the same way.

The children clustered together, then scattered, then swarmed again, like kittens chasing a leaf or a feather. This giant cat had peacefully watched Fort Washakie children play like this for many seasons.

The ball they chased flew toward the big tree, and the laughing children drifted along with it. Above, the old lion shifted to see them better. Her movement caught the eye of one little girl. Then the whistle blew and recess was over.

Back in the classroom, it was time for Centers. At the Writing Center, Billi whispered to her best friend, Blaze. "Did you see the big kitty?"

"Huh, what kitty?" he whispered back.

"Up in the big tree."

"Nope. Where?" Blaze asked. "Show me."

They left their table to look out the window. The tree was just out of sight.

"Billi and Blaze," called Nadine. "You know what we are doing now. Please . . ."

"I'll show you at lunchtime," Billi promised. "But it's our secret."

Later, the two smiling friends and the big kitty spent part of lunch recess quietly watching each other. The lion seemed to smile, too.

"She has been here before," Billi whispered as she and Blaze lay looking up into the branches. "My big brother, Jessie, told me about her."

"You have a brother?" Blaze was surprised.

"He lives with his dad in Riverton now." Billi answered. "He's in sixth grade."

"When Jessie would talk about the lion at home," she said quietly, "Grandmother told him not to tell others. She said the lion was watching over us."

Before afternoon recess, Nadine asked Mrs. LeClerq if she thought Blaze and Billi were acting strange. "Do you think they are getting sick? They didn't play after lunch. They just lay down under the tree while everyone else played ball."

"Hmmm, I didn't notice that," replied Nadine's mentor. "I'll keep an eye on them. It would be a shame if they missed any school this late in the year."

When Mrs. LeClerq watched Billi and Blaze under the tree later that afternoon, her sight followed theirs into the branches. She saw the giant cat and quietly herded the children to the basketball court farthest from the tree. Then she walked quickly to the office.

Very soon there were uniformed men and women—Tribal Police, Game and Fish, and County Sheriff staff—on the playground. They looked out of place with the rifles they carried and the pistol belts around their waists. All of them stood looking into the cottonwood's lower branches.

They gestured little with their hands. Only the white man in the County Sheriff's outfit pointed with his fingers.

Billi, Blaze, and all the kindergarteners already knew that Indians pointed with their chins. This movement is much less noticeable to animals and enemies than raising arms and hands.

Billi stood by her teacher and asked what the people in uniforms were going to do. "They are deciding how to get that big mountain lion away from here," said Mrs. LeClerq. "So that we will be safe. Lions can eat children."

Billi knew about guns. She ran over to the strangers. "Don't shoot her. She's an old gramma lion," she said in a quiet voice.

The big people looked down, surprised to see such a little person. "We don't want to hurt her," said a lady in a greenish shirt and pants.

"But she is a danger to you kids," piped up a big man who seemed to want to be in charge. He cradled a scoped rifle in the crook of his arm. "I say one shot from this will bring her down dead. Problem solved. Safely."

He looked at Mrs. LeClerq. "Ma'am, will you get these kids out of here?" He ordered, adding, "Please." The word didn't sound polite.

Nadine helped lead the class back into the school while the people in uniforms debated loudly. Some wanted to tranquilize and transport the lion. The rest voted for killing. Through all the talk, their subject up in the branches lay still and unconcerned.

Inside the school, children watched from every window as a shot shocked the air. Then another. Then another. And no lion fell.

As the buses began pulling away, taking everyone home for the night, a long ladder was brought to the big tree and the big Tribal Policeman began to climb. Teachers and staff watched as he respectfully climbed down with the dead lion over one shoulder.

He lay the old lion down gently on the grass while two of the officers assessed their shooting accuracy. They talked with each other, puzzled looks on all their faces. Finally, one spoke loud enough for Mrs. LeClerq and the others to hear.

"This is one for the books," the Game

and Fish officer said as he crouched down over the body. "She's cold as can be. This lion died hours ago," he said softly and thoughtfully. "She just came and climbed up to watch the children one more time. Curiosity . . ."

SIX

Counting Noses

Heidi Teagan is now an excellent grade-school teacher, but during her college years she served in the U.S. Forest Service. For seven summers she worked in the Wyoming wilderness and had many humorous and harrowing adventures. Some involved people. Some involved weather. Some involved animals. Some of the animals were mountain lions. One of these was both the most humorous and most harrowing adventure. I will let her tell this story.

Heidi began with a weary tone to her voice. "You remember the summers when we worked together with the Back

Country Horsemen clearing and building trails in the Platte Ridge Wilderness. You guys did a lot of good—when you showed up," she added with a wry smile.

"Well, near the end of those summers . . . when I started thinking of packing up for the peace of winter, the 'Golfers' and their families showed up for the four-day Annual Long-Weekend Pasture Pool Tournament.

"These guys were mostly professors from the university in Laramie, but they could have been circus people on vacation. Their clothes were like circus costumes, anyway. They acted more like clowns than college profs. I guess they came to Douglas Creek early every August to blow off steam between summer school and the fall semester.

"The first couple of summers they visited, I was amazed and amused. They set up five or six big tents in their camp next to the creek near the 'golf course.' That was the first big meadow you come to along the trail, once you are into the wilderness area.

"Once the camp was set up, they went to marking off their nine-hole golf course. It was a big area and all of it 'rough.' Then they got out their 'clubs.' Clubs were huge replicas of civilized golf clubs—more like polo or long-handled croquet mallets. For golf balls, they used plastic softball-sized balls colored Day-Glo orange, pink, or lime green. The bright colors helped them find the balls in the tall grass.

"There was lots of entertainment

besides the 'tournament.' Each golfer brought the family—kids between two and sixteen in age. Imagine twenty-five rowdy city people and two or three of their yappy pet dogs in a peaceful wilderness where normally only the sounds of wind in the trees and water in the creek reach the ears of animals!

"The golfers took good care of the meadow and camp area. But the noise they made disturbed things.

"In fact, their noisiness is what drew the big cat to them. You know that the high-pitched voices and darting awkwardness of little kids and dogs is stimulating to predators.

"The golfing troupe brought another attractive item. The scent of meat also draws bears, coyotes, and cougars. The golfers always finished their outing with a pig roast. The 'dressed-out' pig—along with a modest quantity of beer and wine—was kept cool beside the camp in the chill waters of Douglas Creek for two days before the roasting began.

"Now, I can't say for sure where the invisible lion was when the golfers arrived. But I can imagine she was with her two cubs, high in the rocks and cliffs around Devil's Gate, growing nervously curious about the intruders below.

"I can say for pretty sure what she did once she was aware of the ruckus in the meadow below. I can say for absolutely sure that the meat and kid-noise aroused her interest."

Here, Heidi stopped to teach me.

"Mountain lions get a bad rap from

know-nothing people. They aren't man-eaters. Since the 1890s, in Mexico, the U.S., and Canada, there were seventy deadly attacks on humans recorded. Less than one a year. About half of these deaths were children.

"Seventy fatal cougar attacks in 125 years! Tim, you are more likely to be killed by lightning or your own dog than by a mountain lion.

"Still, if you know anything and you are in lion country, you take precautions. My golfers knew enough, but were plumb careless anyway."

Her lesson over, Heidi continued.

"After dusk, but before the rustler's moon was high in the sky, mama lion led her cubs to a rocky shelter in the pines above the camp along the Douglas. From there, she watched and listened and, I imagine, taught her young ones lessons about 'two-leggeds.'

"Gradually, the voices and noises in the camp grew quiet. Somewhere near two thirty in the morning, she gave her cubs the silent command to 'stay,' and glided between the boulders and trees at the edge of the sage-dappled meadow, toward the tents.

"An unfamiliar but tempting scent in the chilly air drew her to the water. The young slaughtered pig was tied with ropes and weighted with large rocks. She moved like smoke along the bank and came to the pig without making a ripple in the water.

"A sniff and a lick told her that this was good. She took hold with her teeth and dragged on the carcass. In seconds, her 130 pounds of hard, straining muscle tore the rope from its anchor, and the lion was away downstream, toward the hiding place where the young lions waited. They had feasted on the carcass, hidden the remaining half, and were safely back in their rocky den by morning.

"That is where I come into the story. I was bringing out some of my gear, leading my Appy pack horse, Annie, remember her?" I nodded yes.

"I could hear the shouting and cussing from a mile away on the ridge above the Douglas. There was anger in the voices, but not alarm. So, I was expecting what I found.

"As soon as I was noticed—about

fifty yards from the tents—a gaggle of shouting, arm-waving golfers, partners, and children trotted toward me in a fog of dust, all protesting at once.

"'We've been robbed! There are thieves out here! Somebody snuck in here last night and stole our roasting pig! That was our farewell feast for tonight.'

"'Better show me,' I said, as calm as I could be facing the agitated gang of duffers and families. 'Where was this pig being kept?'

"I dropped Annie's lead rope and rode to the creek beside the trotting, whining campers.

"I got down from my saddle. 'Okay,' I said, 'Have you walked the creek bed? The current didn't carry it away?'

"A graying fellow stepped up and

pointed downstream. (He had enormous hands.) 'Walked it for a hundred yards to the quiet pool. Not a sign.'

"'Any beverages missing?'

"'Nope, they left that alone,' another voice replied. Then I saw and nodded toward the big M-shaped track at water level. 'Have you counted noses? Where are pets and children?'

"The air took on an icy chill. Anger on faces turned to worry. Angry voices went silent as mothers and fathers gathered their kids and canines.

"Well, it turned out that all were present and accounted for, as they nearly always are when lions intrude on human activities. Memories of life in the realm of the big cat were recalled and retold that day and night. The group was sobered.

No one complained about the campfire feast that evening. Dishes like Spam, spaghetti, and mac and cheese were more than satisfying to the families that huddled around that fire."

SEVEN

Getting Along

I began this little book by telling you about my only experience with America's big cat. Frankly, I was both awestruck and alarmed. That mountain lion matched my size, but he was all muscle and agility, with huge teeth and claws. He had disappeared in the second or two it took me to call Alice to the window and turn back toward him.

But all I knew was legend learned from the cowboy movies I grew up with. I knew he could run fast and jump high. I did not know he could cover ground in bounds of forty feet. I didn't know he could leap to a rooftop fifteen feet above while carrying a fawn deer. I believe the lion I saw "disappeared" in just that way. And when I walked outside the cabin, he could have dropped down on me.

But what I have learned in the last months tells me I was safe. Mountain lions almost never attack humans.

Last week, I visited the ranch again. I asked, "Got any good lion stories?" I expected to hear that hunters or trappers had come and "removed" the dangerous predators. But that is not what I was told.

The ranch manager reached for his smartphone and showed me pictures of two young lions walking through falling snow outside the ranch kitchen. The two were half-grown and still had the spotted coats they were born with.

Next morning, the ranch chef, a guy called Lefty, told me that the lions had been good neighbors. "We bring our pets in at night," he said, picking up his orange Garfield cat. "But the lions are mainly invisible and peaceful toward us.

"We try to understand and get along. After all, their kind were here long before the 1890s when this place was built," he said, looking out at the hay meadow, cottonwood groves, and fast-running Laramie River.

I was surprised at first that the mountain lion sightings a year ago had not led to their extermination. At least, I thought, the big male I had seen and the others, in the woods, would have been trapped and taken far, far away.

I knew that landowners were permitted to kill large predators that threatened their livestock—mainly cattle and sheep. The ranch where I visited was home to horses. The manager and wranglers seemed to think that there was no reason to remove their *Puma concolor* population.

"So," I said, "Tell me about the year with the lions."

Lefty gave me an honest look. "Not much to tell. Those pictures you saw last night show the only sighting since last summer. We find the deer the mountain lions have fed on. That's how we know they are about. But nobody here has seen a single paw print. It is hard to call it coexistence, when you aren't sure you have neighbors."

CPSIA information can be obtained
at www.ICGtesting.com
Printed in the USA
LVHW03s0029060818
586084LV00001B/5/P

9 781936 846535